PUFFIN BOOKS

KING KEITH AND THE NASTY CASE
OF DRAGONITUS

King Keith has a right royal cold and is making everyone in
the palace suffer for it. He moans, groans and bosses them
around until they're totally worn out. And he won't take his
medicine, because he thinks it will taste nasty. How will he be
persuaded? Then, a spotty dragon with the dreaded Dragonitus enters town and King Keith is suddenly forced to take
drastic action.

King Keith and his cousin, King Clive, have never got on.
Whatever King Keith does, Cousin Clive does it better. Cousin
Clive has a flashier coach, a bigger palace and stacks of money.
One day, disaster strikes. Cousin Clive invites himself to tea at
King Keith's. The whole palace is in a panic to prepare for
Cousin Clive's visit, except for King Keith, who is in a right
royal sulk. Will Cousin Clive and King Keith finally be able to
settle old scores?

Apart from writing children's books, Kaye Umansky has been
a drama teacher, a TV presenter for educational programmes
and has also sung in a band! She is married with one daughter
and lives in London.

Also by Kaye Umansky

BIG IGGY
THE FWOG PWINCE
PONGWIFFY
TRASH HITS
WITCHES IN STITCHES

KAYE UMANSKY

KING KEITH AND THE
NASTY CASE
OF DRAGONITUS

ILLUSTRATED BY AINSLIE MACLEOD

PUFFIN BOOKS

PUFFIN BOOKS

Published by the Penguin Group
Penguin Books Ltd, 27 Wrights Lane, London W8 5TZ, England
Viking Penguin, a division of Penguin Books USA Inc.
375 Hudson Street, New York, New York 10014, USA
Penguin Books Australia Ltd, Ringwood, Victoria, Australia
Penguin Books Canada Ltd, 2801 John Street, Markham, Ontario, Canada L3R 1B4
Penguin Books (NZ) Ltd, 182–190 Wairau Road, Auckland 10, New Zealand

Penguin Books Ltd, Registered Offices: Harmondsworth, Middlesex, England

First published by Viking 1990
Published in Puffin Books 1991
10 9 8 7 6 5 4 3 2 1

Text copyright © Kaye Umansky, 1990
Illustrations copyright © Ainslie MacLeod, 1990
All rights reserved

The moral right of the author and illustrator has been asserted

Printed in England by Clays Ltd, St Ives plc
Filmset in Linotron Palatino

Contents

King Keith
and the Nasty Case
of Dragonitus

The Royal Cold

King Keith had a right royal cold. He sneezed and wheezed. His throat hurt. He lay in his bed shouting for this and that. When they brought him this, he wanted that. When they brought him that, he wanted something altogether different. He moaned and groaned and bossed and bullied until everyone was worn out. Queen Freda finally got so tired of him that she sent for the Royal Doctor.

"Your Majesty! It's me, Doctor Coldfingers. Can I come in?" called the doctor, knocking on the door.

"NO!" snapped King Keith. "Go away. I don't want a doctor. Tell the cook to bring me chocolate ice-cream. Atchoo!"

"Rubbish," said Doctor Coldfingers, going in anyway. "The last thing you need is chocolate ice-cream. I know because I'm a doctor."

"Oh really?"

King Keith glared at Doctor Coldfingers over his hot-water bottle. "So what *do* I need, Coldfingers? In your opinion?"

"Medicine," said Doctor Coldfingers firmly, producing a large bottle of something green and nasty looking from behind his back.

"Oh no I don't," said King Keith.

"Oh yes you do. Open up."

"No," said King Keith and dived under the pillows.

"Come out, Your Majesty, and drink your medicine like a brave king," coaxed Doctor Coldfingers.

"Go away," said King Keith.

Just then, Queen Freda came in. Her nose was very red and sore looking.

"Good morning, doctor. Good morning, dearest," said Queen Freda. "Look, I've picked you a bunch of tulips. They're the ones you planted yourself in the town square. How is your cold?"

"Atchoo! Terrible. Did you send for him?" growled King Keith, pointing at Doctor Coldfingers.

"I most certainly did."

"Why? I don't want him. I don't like doctors."

"But dearest, you must get rid of your cold. You're giving it to everyone in the palace. It's very selfish of you. Atchoo! Drink the medicine, there's a dear."

"No," said King Keith. "Never. I hate medicine. It tastes nasty."

"But you haven't even tried it. Look, I'll take a spoonful."

Queen Freda opened her mouth. Doctor

Coldfingers unscrewed the bottle and tipped it up. The green nasty stuff oozed into the spoon with a glopping noise, and Queen Freda swallowed it. She made a little face, but that was all.

"There. That wasn't so bad. Now you."

"Shan't," said King Keith. And closed his lips tight together.

Just then Prince Percy came into the room, blowing his nose loudly.

"Hello, dad," said Prince Percy. "How are

you feeling?"

"He won't take his medicine," sighed Queen Freda.

"He thinks it tastes nasty," said Doctor Coldfingers.

"I'll try it," said Prince Percy. "I think I've caught his cold." And he took a spoonful.

"Not bad," he said. "Now you, dad."

"No," sulked King Keith. "I don't like the colour. I want chocolate ice-cream."

At that moment, there was the sound of

sniffing, and Princess Paula came in.

"Why are you shouting, daddy?" complained Princess Paula. "My ears are hurting. I'm sure I've got a cold coming."

"Your father won't take his medicine," said Doctor Coldfingers.

"He thinks it will taste nasty," sighed Queen Freda.

"He doesn't like the colour," said Prince Percy.

"Well!" said Princess Paula. "You great big baby! Look, I'll try some." And she did. "Now you."

"No. It's too thick," said King Keith stubbornly.

"Whad's too thig?" said a voice, and the Lord Chamberlain came into the room. He was talking funny because he too had a very bad cold.

"The King's medicine," said Queen Freda.

"He says it tastes nasty," explained Prince Percy.

"And he doesn't like the colour," added Princess Paula.

"In thad case, he wode mind if I hab sub," said the Lord Chamberlain. "Mmm. Nod too bad. Try it, Your Bajesty."

"No," said King Keith. "I don't like the shape of the bottle. I'm fussy about things like that."

"Isn't he selfish?" sighed Queen Freda. "We've all got colds because of him."

Everyone agreed that King Keith was very selfish.

Just then, the door flew open, and the Royal Messenger came panting in. Now, the Royal Messenger didn't have a cold. He had something worse! In fact, **he was covered from head to foot in green spots!** Everyone gasped. He wasn't usually like that.

"Your Majesty! Bad news!" panted the Royal Messenger. "There's a Dragon in the town square!"

"A DRAGON?" gasped everyone.

"Yes. And what's more, it's got
Dragonitus. Everyone's catching it. The
whole town's coming out in green spots.
And I can tell you, they itch something
rotten!"

"Tell it to go away," ordered King Keith
firmly.

"It won't, sir. It says it feels too ill to move. It's digging a hole to lie down in. All the tulips you planted are getting ruined. Request permission to scratch, sir."

"Permission denied," said King Keith meanly.

"Go and do it outside, you poor man," said Queen Freda kindly, and the Royal Messenger fled.

"Dragonitus," muttered Doctor Coldfingers. "It sounds serious. I wonder if there's a cure? I think I'll go and see the Medicine Maker."

"We'll all come with you," said Queen Freda. "This is a National Emergency. Come along, Keith."

"Not me," said King Keith. "I'm much too ill. Ask the cook to hurry up with my ice-cream, will you?"

And he snuggled down beneath the blankets.

Ludovic Linctus

The Medicine Maker lived in a very odd house on the other side of town. It was made of thick brown glass, and shaped like a huge bottle. There were no windows, but it did have a white round door. On it were written the words:

LUDOVIC LINCTUS
MEDICINE MAKER
KNOCK THREE TIMES AFTER MEALS

As Queen Freda, Percy, Paula, Doctor Coldfingers and the Lord Chamberlain approached, they could see clouds of bright blue smoke puffing from the bottle neck.

Percy and Paula nudged each other excitedly. They had always wanted to see inside the Medicine Maker's house.

Doctor Coldfingers knocked three times.

"Can't you read?" shouted a cross voice from inside. "It says *after* meals. I haven't had breakfast yet."

"It's a National Emergency, Mr Linctus!" called Doctor Coldfingers. "Open up. I've got the Queen and Prince Percy and Princess Paula and the Lord Chamberlain with me!"

After a lot of mumbling, the door finally opened and Ludovic Linctus peered out. He was very old, with a long beard stained all colours of the rainbow. His robe was covered with messy splash marks, and his hands were bright green.

"I can't get the dye off," he explained. "It splashed all over me yesterday when I was making up the medicine for King Keith. Did it help, by the way?"

"The King won't take it, I'm afraid. He's a

terrible baby about taking medicine. But we did, and our colds are much better," said Queen Freda.

"Did you drop the bottle or something?" asked Ludovic Linctus.

"No. Why?"

"Because you're all covered in green spots."

The Queen, the doctor, the Lord Chamberlain, Percy and Paula looked at each other. Sure enough. They were.

"Oh, dear," said Queen Freda. "Dragonitus. We've caught it already. Can we come in?"

"Yes, of course, of course. You'll have to excuse the mess."

They found themselves in a huge round room. The glass walls were lined with shelves holding hundreds of strange potions in bottles of all shapes and sizes. There were tubs of tablets and pots of powders. There were packets of pills and heaps of herbs.

Tables were piled high with old books,

oddly shaped glass instruments and half-eaten sandwiches. In the middle of the floor a large pot of bright blue liquid hissed and bubbled over a fire. Curly blue smoke rose into the bottle-neck chimney high above their heads.

"A National Emergency, you say?" said Ludovic Linctus, giving the pot a little stir.

"Yes. You see, Mr Linctus, there's a sick Dragon in the town square. It's got Dragonitus. Everyone's catching it, and coming out in green spots," explained Doctor Coldfingers. "We're hoping you might know of a cure."

"Dragonitus, eh? Hmm. Just a moment."

The Medicine Maker hobbled over to a tottering pile of ancient books. He picked them up one by one, peered at the faded titles and threw them carelessly over his shoulder any old how. The Queen, the doctor and the Lord Chamberlain had to keep ducking as tatty old volumes flew past their ears. Percy and Paula looked at each other and giggled.

"Ah ha!" shouted Ludovic Linctus, finally finding the one he wanted. "Here we are. RARE RASHES IN REPTILES. Should be in here. Now, let me see. Damp patches – Dandruff – Distemper – Ah! Got it! Dragonitus."

"Is it serious?" asked Queen Freda anxiously, peering over Ludovic Linctus's

shoulder.

"Serious? Oh yes, definitely. Very nasty indeed. It's easier to cure at the green spot stage, of course. It's when the hiccups start it gets more difficult. When the hair starts dropping out and the fingernails turn orange, it's practically impossible. . ."

"But there is a cure?" broke in the Lord Chamberlain, turning pale beneath his spots. "You did say there was a cure?"

"Oh yes. Special medicine. It'll take me some time to make it up, though."

"Can we help?" asked Percy and Paula together.

"If you like. But you need strong stomachs. I warn you, Dragonitus Cure has got some very nasty things in it. Dried moths for a start. And fresh beetle juice. Then there's fish bones and a teaspoon of frog spawn. And a pickled mouse nose. Mustn't forget that."

"I think I'll go back to the palace," said Queen Freda hastily. "I'm going to run a nice warm bath, and see if it will stop this horrid itching."

"Me too," said Doctor Coldfingers. "Could you scratch my back, please, Lord Chamberlain? Just between the shoulder blades."

"We want to stay and help. Oh, please! Can we?" begged Percy and Paula.

"Very well. If you don't get in the way," said Queen Freda. "A pickled mouse nose. Uggh!"

"Right," said Ludovic Linctus as soon as they had gone. "Having two helpers should speed things up a bit. I'm going to write out a list of the things I need, and you're going to find them. Ready?"

"Rather," said Percy and Paula. And they hopped from foot to foot and scratched excitedly while Ludovic Linctus wrote out a list of ingredients.

The Dragon

Meanwhile, King Keith lay in bed feeling
very irritable. He had spent the last hour
shouting and ringing his bell, but nobody
had come. He was bored and hungry. Worst
of all, he was beginning to itch all over. Idly,
he picked up the hand mirror next to his bed
and peered at himself.

Oh no! Big green spots, all over him!

"That's it!" shouted King Keith, throwing
back the bedclothes and reaching for his
Royal robe. "*That is it!* How dare this Dragon
come to my town and get all the attention
and pass on its beastly illness to me, the

King! If nobody else will get rid of it, I'll just have to do it myself."

And up he got, and out he went.

The town was deserted. Everyone was at home, peering in mirrors, rubbing on cream and scratching, scratching, scratching.

As King Keith rounded a corner, a green spotted dog caught sight of itself in a shop window, gave a terrified howl and ran away with its tail between its legs, almost tripping him up.

A green spotted horse came racing down the road, cart rattling behind. It was making for the river, where it could roll in the cool mud. There was no sign of its owner.

Three green spotted pigeons waddled around in the road, pecking crossly at their feathers. They were being watched by a green spotted stray cat, who was busily licking its itchy tail with a green spotted tongue.

"It's a disgrace!" growled King Keith to the cat. "Just you wait till I meet that Dragon. I'll have a few words to say, I can tell you!"

Soon, he reached the town square – or what was left of it. It was really more a big hole than a square. Trees were toppled, all the grass was uprooted and King Keith's prize tulips were lying around all over the place. Huge piles of earth surrounded the hole, and the place looked like a

building site.

King Keith marched up to the edge of the hole and looked down.

A very large, green, spotty, sad face looked back up at him.

"Sorry about this," said the Dragon.

"So you should be," snapped King Keith.

"I don't usually go round digging holes in squares," explained the Dragon. "It's my illness. I feel terrible. You're my first visitor.

I'm so glad you've come, because I've been badly neglected. Have you brought me some grapes?"

The Dragon really didn't look at all well. Nobody had come to see how it was, because they were all in their homes peering in mirrors and scratching at their green spots.

"Grapes? Certainly not. I've come to order you out of my square," shouted King Keith. "What is all this mess? How dare you!"

"Please don't shout. I have this splitting headache," said the Dragon. "Nobody cares that I feel awful. Oh, my poor tummy. Oh, my aching limbs. Oh, my itchy spots."

"*You* feel awful? What about me?" shouted King Keith. "I'll have you know I've had a very bad cold for days. And now I've caught Dragonitus. You've got me out of bed, you have. Don't you know who I am?"

"No," said the Dragon. "But whoever you are, I don't like you much."

"Well, I'm the King, and I give the orders

around here," snapped King Keith haughtily. "I'm going to count to three, and I want you out of my square. Look what you've done to it! What's that hole for anyway? Atchoo!"

"You can count to five thousand if you like," said the Dragon. "It won't make a jot of difference. I'm not going anywhere. I'm too weak to move. The hole is for me to crawl into. We Dragons always crawl into holes when we're not well. I'll try not to be any trouble. All you have to do is fill it in again. When I'm gone." And a big tear rolled down its scaly cheek.

Just then, there was the sound of running footsteps, and Prince Percy and Princess Paula came racing up. Percy was carrying a huge bottle, and Paula held a gigantic spoon. Hobbling behind them came Ludovic Linctus.

"Oh good," said the Dragon. "More visitors. I hope they'll be more sympathetic than you are."

"Dad! Good news! Guess what's in this bottle!"

"Lemonade," said the Dragon. "For my poor sore throat."

"Wrong," said Prince Percy. "It's Dragonitus Cure."

"We helped make it," added Paula. "Daddy, this is Ludovic Linctus, the Medicine Maker. Oh, poor Dragon. You do

look awful."

"I know," said the Dragon. "Tell *him* that," it added, with a bitter glance at King Keith.

"I suppose you're the one who made that revolting cold medicine," said King Keith to Ludovic Linctus. "I refused to drink it."

"Well, that's a pity, Your Majesty. My medicines might taste nasty, but they usually do the trick."

"Let's hope this one works," snapped King Keith, snatching the bottle. "Right. Come along, Dragon. Open up. Time for your medicine."

"NO," said the Dragon, clearly and firmly. "NO."

No

"Did I hear right?" said King Keith. "Did you say NO to the King?"

"Yes," said the Dragon. "No." And it continued to dig, scattering earth and tulips to the four winds.

"Don't be silly," said King Keith. "It's medicine to cure you. It's lovely."

He unscrewed the cap. The smell coming from the bottle was so dreadful he almost stopped breathing. The Dragon watched him suspiciously.

"Mmmm," said King Keith. "What a yummy smell. I wonder if it tastes as good as it smells."

"Only one way of finding out," said the Dragon. "Try it."

"Who, me?" gasped King Keith in horror.

"You," said the Dragon firmly, and crossed its arms.

"Just one moment," said King Keith. "A word in private."

Percy, Paula, Ludovic Linctus and King Keith went into a huddle while the Dragon

returned to its digging.

"What's in this stuff?" asked King Keith suspiciously. Percy and Paula both opened their mouths to tell him. Ludovic Linctus gave them a warning look, and they closed them again.

"Oh – nothing much," said Ludovic Linctus. "This and that. That and this, and a bit of the other. It won't hurt you. In fact, it'll cure your green spots."

"I don't like the look of it," whispered King Keith. "Or the smell."

"You see?" said the Dragon, pausing in its digging. "He doesn't like the look of it."

"Yes I do," fibbed King Keith. "It looks lovely. It smells delicious. *Please* stop that digging, and take your medicine, there's a good – er – lizard."

"You know your trouble?" said the Dragon. "You're scared."

"Don't be ridiculous," spluttered King Keith. "Gracious. Is that the time? I really must be going. . ."

"You see?" said the Dragon. "He's scared to try it. He's a cowardy king."

"Oh no he's not," said Percy and Paula together. "*Are* you, dad?"

"Why doesn't he drink it, then?" taunted the Dragon.

"Oh all right! All right!" screamed King Keith, finally losing patience. "Anything to stop you spoiling my tulips!"

And bravely, with shaking hands, he poured the black mixture into the spoon, took a deep breath, and swallowed. There was a long pause. Everyone stared at him.

"Well?" said the Dragon. "Is it horrible?"

"Not at all," said King Keith, crossing his fingers behind his back. It was the worst thing he had ever tasted in his life. A sort of cross between dried moths, beetle juice, fish bones, powdered stinging nettles, chopped toadstools and a pickled mouse nose.

"Your turn now," he added.

"No," said the Dragon, flopping into the hole and sending showers of earth and broken tulips high into the air. "I don't like the colour."

"Why not? It's a lovely colour."

"Have some more, then," jeered the Dragon, still digging.

"Mustn't be greedy," said poor King Keith. "Somebody else."

"You," said the Dragon, peering over the
edge.

"Oh – very well. If I must." And King
Keith poured out another spoonful, closed
his eyes and swallowed, trying very hard to
think of chocolate ice-cream.

"Awful, isn't it?" said the Dragon. "I
know it is."

"No. I've told you, it's quite disgus . . .
delicious," spluttered King Keith bravely.

"Daddy," said Paula. "Your spots are fading!" And so they were.

"There, you see? It works," said King Keith. "Come on, Dragon. Your turn now."

"No," said the Dragon stubbornly. "I don't like the shape of the bottle."

The hole was very deep now, and the mound of earth was beginning to look like a mountain.

"Go on, Dragon," coaxed Paula. "Be brave. You want to get better, don't you?"

"I'll do it if he has one more spoonful," said the Dragon. Everyone looked hopefully at King Keith.

"Oh well," he said.

"Here goes," he said.

And he took one more spoonful.

Percy, Paula and Ludovic Linctus clapped their hands. He had been so very brave.

"All right," said the Dragon in a sulky voice. "If I've *got* to."

King Keith carefully poured out a

spoonful of the Dragonitus Cure. Prince
Percy and Princess Paula reached into the
hole and held the Dragon's nose. The huge
mouth opened – and –

"Yuck! Groooooooer! Ugggy uggy ugggh!"
choked the Dragon.

"Keep holding his nose!" shouted Ludovic
Linctus. "He's got to have three!"

"Quite right," agreed King Keith. "After
all, I had to. Here goes with the second!"

"Yeeeeeeeeeeeeuck! Blurk. Oooooooer,"
moaned the Dragon, thrashing its tail. "No
more! No more!"

"Last one coming up," said King Keith.
"Be brave." And down it went.

Everyone drew back with a sigh of relief.
The Dragon choked, coughed and wiped its
eyes.

"Look!" shouted Percy. "Its spots are
fading!"

And sure enough, they were.

"I must admit I do feel much better,"

admitted the Dragon. "In fact, I think I'm strong enough to move away from this square now. I'm sorry about the tulips. Thanks for the medicine. It tasted awful, but it did me good. Oh well. Back to the volcano. Goodbye." And off it lumbered, doing a little skip as it went.

"Dad," said Prince Percy. "You were wonderful." And Princess Paula gave him a big kiss. "We're so proud of you," she said.

"What a stubborn creature," said King Keith, shaking his head.

"Like someone else I could mention," said Ludovic Linctus with a little smile. King Keith looked cross, then ashamed, then, finally, he laughed.

"Ludovic Linctus," he said. "You're right. I suppose I was being unreasonable. But I've certainly paid for it. That was the worst thing I've ever tasted in my life."

"I'm sorry, Your Majesty. I was in a hurry, you see. When I make some more for everybody, it'll be chocolate ice-cream flavoured. If anything can hide the taste of dried moths, beetle juice, frog spawn, fish bones, chopped toadstools, a pickled mouse nose and powdered stinging nettles, it's chocolate."

King Keith went very pale. Finally, he managed a little smile. Then he gave a little wave, and began to walk away.

"Where are you going, daddy?" called Princess Paula.

"Home to take my cold medicine," said King Keith. "After Dragonitus Cure, I can drink anything!"

And that was that.

King Keith and
Cousin Clive

Bad News

"Oh no!" said King Keith to Queen Freda, Prince Percy, Princess Paula, the Lord Chamberlain and Doctor Coldfingers. They were all sitting around the kitchen table eating breakfast, and King Keith was reading his morning post in between mouthfuls of boiled egg. "Oh dear! Oh bother! Oh blow!"

"What is it, dearest? Bad news?" asked Queen Freda, spreading jam on her toast.

"It's a letter from my cousin, King Clive. Listen. *Dear Cousin Keith. As we haven't seen each other for ten years, I thought I would call in and visit you on Saturday afternoon at three o'clock.* That's this afternoon! Oh, what a disaster!"

"Why? What's so terrible about that?" asked Queen Freda.

"It's very nice to be visited by relations," nodded the Lord Chamberlain.

"It depends on the relation," said King Keith gloomily. "If the relation is Clive, it's not nice at all."

"Why?" everyone asked curiously.

"Because he's a great big show-off, that's why. He's always boasting about things. *My* palace is bigger than *your* palace. *My* coach is bigger than *your* coach. *I* get more pocket money than *you* do. He's always been like that, even when we were little. The first words he ever spoke to me were: *My* rattle's bigger than *your* rattle."

"Was it?" asked Percy and Paula together.

"Well, yes, as a matter of fact. But mine was louder. And I made it myself, with a squeezy bottle."

"Well done, Your Majesty," said Doctor Coldfingers admiringly. "You're so clever at making things yourself."

"All his things were better than mine," continued King Keith bitterly. "His kite flew higher. His ball bounced higher. Everything we got, his had to be bigger and grander. Even his teddy wore a crown."

"Keith, you're being ridiculous," said Queen Freda.

"Ah, but you haven't heard about the business of the tree houses," said King Keith, getting into his stride. "You see, I built this tree house. I did it all by myself with my Junior King Carpentry Set. Then Clive came along, and had another one built on the branch next to mine. His had four rooms and fitted carpets. And running water and a proper stove that worked. It made mine look really silly."

"Poor dad," chorused Percy and Paula

sympathetically.

"So now you see why I don't like Clive," finished King Keith. "I stopped being friends with him ten years ago, and we haven't spoken since."

"Then it's time you made it up," said Queen Freda briskly. "Rattles! Tree houses! What nonsense. I'm sure King Clive has forgotten all about them. I'll ask Cook to prepare a special tea. With iced buns."

"And sausage rolls?" asked Percy.

"Certainly sausage rolls," said Queen Freda.

"And jam tarts?" asked Paula.

"Jam tarts of course," said Queen Freda.

"And red jelly?" muttered King Keith, coming round a little.

"Definitely red jelly," nodded Queen Freda. "In fact, we'll make it a proper party. You can cut some flowers for the table, Keith. Roses, I think. The red ones."

"I'm not picking my prize blooms for

Clive," said King Keith stubbornly. He was very proud of his prize rose-bush.

"Oh yes you are," said Queen Freda firmly. "King Clive is a visitor, and we're going to give him a proper welcome. Fancy not speaking to someone for ten years. I've never heard of such a thing. Keith, I want your solemn word that you will be polite."

"No," said King Keith. "Shan't. Don't like him."

"Oh, go on dad," said Prince Percy.

"Ten years is a long time," said Princess Paula.

"You should give him another chance, Your Majesty," urged the Lord Chamberlain and Doctor Coldfingers.

"Your solemn promise, Keith," said Queen Freda. "Or no red jelly."

King Keith *loved* red jelly.

"Oh – all right. But he'd better not mention rattles."

"Good," said Queen Freda. "That's

settled. Now, there's lots to do, and we must all help. Percy and Paula, I shall give you a list, and you must pop along to the shops. The palace must be cleaned, of course, and then I must help Cook with the tea. Keith, after you've picked the roses you can cut the hedge straight. That's the first thing Cousin Clive will notice. Oh dear, I knew we should have decorated this year. Everything looks so tatty. Now then. I wonder where I put the red carpet?"

"Red carpet?" snapped King Keith. "Surely we're not putting out the red carpet for Clive? He doesn't deserve it, Freda. Not after the business of the Go-Carts."

"Just go and pick the roses, Keith," sighed Queen Freda.

"But if I tell you about the Go-Carts, you'll see what I mean. You see, I made this Go-Cart, and Clive. . ."

"Not another word, Keith! The roses!"
King Keith scowled and said no more.

Preparations

The whole morning was spent preparing for
Cousin Clive's visit. Percy and Paula were
sent to the shops at least a dozen times.
Queen Freda set to work with cloths, mops
and buckets. The Lord Chamberlain chased
the dogs and cats off the sofas, and tried
to pick all the hairs from the cushions. Doctor
Coldfingers rubbed at stains on the carpet.
In the Royal Kitchen, the Cook got hot,
cross and bothered as sauces boiled over
and jellies refused to set. Everywhere there
was rubbing and scrubbing and brushing
and fussing.

Through it all, King Keith sulked. He just sat on his throne and swung his legs and sulked. Until Queen Freda saw him, and ordered him into the garden, where he sulked as he picked the roses and cut the hedge.

"Huh!" he thought crossly. "All this fuss for Cousin Clive. I didn't like him then, and I won't like him now. I shall be polite, but I certainly shan't be friendly."

By lunch-time, everyone was quite worn out, particularly King Keith, because

sulking is very tiring.

It would be nice to report that after all that effort, the palace looked lovely. Well, it certainly looked *better* – but Queen Freda was right. It did need decorating. The carpets still had stains, and the wallpaper still dangled in strips where the cats had scratched it. There were still those high, round, dirty marks on the wall where Percy and Paula had kicked the football. King Keith's throne still wobbled when you sat on it, and the bath plug still didn't fit properly.

"Oh well. We've done our best," sighed Queen Freda.

"Can we have lunch now?" begged King Keith. "There are all those little sausage rolls. . ."

"Certainly not," said Queen Freda. "Those are for tea. We've just got time to wash and put our best clothes on. Clive is due at three o'clock, and we have to be on the steps ready to greet him. And, Keith. Remember, you promised. You be nice to him."

At exactly three o'clock, washed, scrubbed and feeling very smart in their best clothes, everyone gathered on the palace steps. The red carpet was in place. It was rather threadbare, and had some nasty marks on it, but as the Lord Chamberlain pointed out, it was the thought that counted.

"You've made a disgraceful job of that hedge, Keith dear," remarked Queen Freda.

"What did you use? Your teeth?"

Even King Keith had to admit that the hedge was rather uneven.

"But it doesn't really matter," he added gloomily. "I don't know why we've bothered at all, really. However hard we try, it won't be good enough for Clive. You don't know how awful he is. Why, once, he even. . ."

But he didn't get any further.

"Sssssssh!" hissed Queen Freda. "Stand up straight, Percy and Paula. Straighten your

stethoscope, Doctor Coldfingers. Smile,
Keith. Here he comes."

Sure enough, down the long driveway
came a coach. But *what* a coach! It was pulled
by two haughty looking horses. Their silken
reins were held by a stuck-up looking coachman in red velvet livery. It was encrusted
with precious stones, and the door handles
were made of solid gold. There were twiddly,
fiddly bits and swirly, twirly bits. The royal
crest was everywhere. The number-plate

read CLIVE 1.

The coach clattered to a halt, and the stuck-up looking coachman played a solemn fanfare on a trumpet, climbed down, walked to the door and threw it open with a flourish.

"His Majesty King Clive, long may He reign," announced the stuck-up looking coachman, and bowed deeply.

"Huh," said King Keith. "See what I mean? Swankpot."

Out stepped Cousin Clive. Percy and Paula's eyes grew round as he stepped down. Everything about him was so glamorous. Huge rings sparkled on his fingers, and his crown was so tall and splendid that it made King Keith's crown look like something from a Christmas cracker. Suddenly, everybody looked down at their own clothes, and felt horribly underdressed.

Cousin Clive stared down at his feet, wearing the sort of expression people wear when they've stepped in something.

"Oh dear," whispered Queen Freda. "He's noticing the stains on the carpet."

"Hello there, Keith!" boomed Cousin Clive, strutting across and slapping King Keith on the back. "Long time no see. Still wearing the same old crown, I see. I say, old boy, time you got a new carpet, isn't it? Next time I'll bring my own, I've got stacks of it at home. Best quality, of course."

"Hello, Clive," said King Keith stiffly. "This is Queen Freda. And Prince Percy and Princess Paula. And the Lord Chamberlain. And Doctor Coldfingers."

"Pleased to meet you," said King Clive. "Glad you didn't bother to dress up on my account. What d'you think of the new coach, eh? Bought it yesterday. Like it so much, I've ordered another two."

"It's very nice, Cousin Clive," said Queen Freda politely. "Isn't it, Keith?"

"I suppose so," said King Keith. "If you like that sort of thing," he added.

"Oh, I do, I do. Only the very best will do for me. So this is your little palace, eh? Of course, I prefer something bigger myself, but then, I can afford it. I love spending money, don't you? Oh, that reminds me. I've bought you all presents. Coachman! Bring the presents!"

The coachman brought the presents. They were beautifully gift-wrapped in gold paper. Queen Freda got a gold necklace. Percy got a gold belt buckle. Paula got a gold bracelet. The Lord Chamberlain got a gold pen. Doctor Coldfingers got a golden thermometer case. And King Keith got a book on gardening.

"It's very kind of you, Cousin Clive," said Queen Freda. "But you really shouldn't have spent so much money."

"Oh pooh! Money? That stuff? I've got more than I know what to do with," boasted Cousin Clive. "I think you'll enjoy the book, Keith," he added. "Your garden's a mess. Who cut the hedge like that? You need a new

gardener. I've got a whole team of them back home. Where's the swimming pool?"

"I don't have a swimming pool," said King Keith sulkily.

"*No swimming pool? I've got two. One hot, one cold. What about your maze? Surely you've got a maze?*"

"No maze," said King Keith, even more sulkily.

"Amazing! Or should I say, *No* mazing, ha, ha, ha. All right, then, tell me this. *Have you got your own boating lake?* No? I have. I've got an orchard too. What about a waterfall? I'm having one fitted. . ."

"Er – Keith, why don't you take Clive for a

stroll round the garden?" suggested Queen Freda hastily. "Then you can show him exactly what we *have* got. He might be interested in your prize rose-bush."

"I doubt it," said Cousin Clive "You can't beat me for rose growing. I've won every prize for rose growing there is. But yes, by all means, show me round your little garden, old chap. It shouldn't take long, ha, ha, ha. Tell you what, let's all go, eh? And I'll tell you about the new palace I've bought this year."

"Er – I must just pop in and see about tea," said Queen Freda.

"If you'll excuse me, I have to write a letter," said the Lord Chamberlain.

"I must see to my patients," said Doctor Coldfingers.

"Percy and I have some homework to do," said Princess Paula.

And everyone vanished, leaving King Keith to show Cousin Clive round the garden all on his own.

He showed Clive the rockery (which he had built himself). Clive said he had a much bigger one, and the rocks had veins of real gold running through them. He showed Clive the bird table (which he had made himself). Clive said *his* bird table had a roof with a chimney that smoked. He showed him the home-made sundial. Clive said that *his* sundial was a new type with moving hands. He showed him his prize rose-bush. Clive said it was all right, but he was sure he detected a touch of blackspot.

King Keith gritted his teeth and bore it. After all, he had promised that he would be polite. But he was very relieved when he heard the tea bell. He was beginning to crack under the strain.

Tea

"Do you always eat in the kitchen?"
enquired Cousin Clive as they sat round the
table. "At home, I have a choice of three
dining-rooms with crystal chandeliers. Two
sugars, please, Queen Freda. What's for tea?
I'm starving."

What there was for tea was this:
sandwiches, sausage rolls, cheese and
pineapple on sticks, crisps, chocolate
fingers, swiss roll, jam tarts, trifle, ice-
cream, jelly, and three sorts of cake.

Cousin Clive kept bragging about his new
French cook, whose speciality was cold

cauliflower sprinkled with sunflower seeds. But everyone noticed that he kept eating while he talked, and seemed to put away more than anyone.

"Well, that wasn't bad," said Cousin Clive, scraping the last of the cream cake off the plate with his finger. "Of course, I'm used to very different sort of food at home. My French chef cooks this wonderful dish of dandelion leaves and mustard. . ."

"Huh," sniffed Cook, clattering dishes loudly in the sink.

"It sounds awful," said King Keith, suddenly unable to contain himself. "Dandelion leaves and mustard. Yuck."

"I can assure you, old chap, it's delicious," said Cousin Clive, sounding rather hurt.

"I'm sure it is. Don't be rude, Keith. Do go on, Cousin Clive," said Queen Freda politely.

"Thank you. As I was saying, he takes these dandelion leaves. . ."

"Er – excuse me, I have to see a man about a desk," said the Lord Chamberlain hastily.

"Paula and I have to feed the goldfish," said Prince Percy.

"I have to write a prescription," said Doctor Coldfingers.

"I think I'll have an early night," said King Keith.

"Nonsense, Keith. You show Clive round the palace while I help Cook with the dishes," said Queen Freda. "I'm sure you two have a lot to talk about."

So King Keith showed Cousin Clive round the palace. He showed him the throne room. Clive said he had a bigger one, and his throne didn't wobble. He showed him the bathroom. Clive said that he had a better one, with marble tiles and gold-plated taps and a plug that fitted. He showed him the treasury. Clive remarked that it was a very small one, and that *his* treasury was much better stocked. Wherever they went, he noticed the stains on the carpets and the grubby wallpaper. He noticed every chip on the paintwork. He pointed and sneered and criticized until King Keith could stand it no more.

He was just about to lose his temper, when Cousin Clive announced that it was time he was going. Everyone came to the front door to wave him goodbye.

"Thank you," said Cousin Clive. "I've had a very pleasant time, old chap. You must all come to my palace and have tea with me next Saturday."

And off he went, before anyone could think of a good excuse.

Cousin Clive's Place

The following Saturday, at exactly three o'clock on the dot, King Keith, Queen Freda, Prince Percy, Princess Paula, the Lord Chamberlain and Doctor Coldfingers stood before the imposing front door of Cousin Clive's palace.

"Goodness," hissed Princess Paula, pulling the bell rope. "He certainly wasn't exaggerating."

Indeed, none of them had ever seen such a splendid palace. It made King Keith's palace look like a heap of old rubble. It glittered and shone in the sunshine. Brightly coloured flags fluttered from the turrets. Prize roses grew in the window boxes, and signposts pointed the way to the swimming pools, the orchard, the maze, the boating lake and so on.

A butler came to the front door. He looked them up and down haughtily. Everyone had bought new clothes for the occasion, and up to now had thought of themselves as looking rather good.

"Wrong door," said the butler. "The tradesmen's entrance is round the back."

"We've come to tea," explained Queen Freda. "King Clive invited us. We're relatives."

"I see," said the butler, looking as though he didn't believe a word. "Wipe your feet and follow me. And kindly don't touch anything."

And he stalked off down a long, winding corridor. King Keith, Queen Freda, Prince Percy and Princess Paula shuffled along behind, whispering in hushed voices. Their footsteps echoed on the cold marble floors. Grim-faced ancestors stared at them from the walls. Silent servants rustled in and out of doorways, and highly polished suits of armour glared at them from shadowy corners.

"It's not a *cosy* sort of place, is it?" hissed Percy to Paula. And Paula agreed that it wasn't.

"His Majesty is in the throne room," said the butler, stopping and throwing open a door. "Your poor relations, sire," he announced, and stood aside.

The throne room was *vast*. It was so big, it made Cousin Clive look positively minute.

He was seated on a massive, ruby-studded throne, and he held a gigantic golden fob watch in his hand. He waved merrily as King Keith, Queen Freda and Percy and Paula walked in.

"Hah! Three o'clock on the dot. Welcome,

everyone. What do you think of the throne, Keith? Notice it doesn't wobble, ha ha? Now, what would you like to do first? Shall I show you round the place? We've got an hour or two before tea."

And for the next two hours, Cousin Clive showed them round the palace. He showed them the swimming pools, the rockery, the maze, the orchard, the fountain, the bird table, the boating lake, the prize roses and

the coach house where he kept his fleet of coaches. He showed them the first, second and third dining-rooms. He showed them the green bedroom, the blue bedroom, the purple bedroom, the pink bedroom, the white bedroom, the turquoise bedroom and, lastly, the gold bedroom (his).

He showed them the treasury, and insisted they have a go at throwing pound coins around. He showed them his model-making room and his library. He showed them the bathroom, and demonstrated how well the plug fitted.

"It's all lovely, Cousin Clive," said Queen Freda politely. "Isn't it, Keith?"

"I suppose so," muttered King Keith. "If you like that sort of thing." He hoped tea wouldn't be long.

It wasn't.

"Tea," announced Cousin Clive, and threw open the door to one of the cold, echoing dining-rooms. Silverware glittered on a long, polished table. "Cold cauliflower. I think you're going to like it, old chap."

King Keith took one look at the cold grey splodge heaped on his plate, and knew he wouldn't. He folded his arms and looked stubborn.

"Eat it, Keith," hissed Queen Freda.

"No," said King Keith.

"What's the matter, old chap?" enquired Cousin Clive. "Don't you like it?"

And then it happened. King Keith cracked.

"No," said King Keith. "I don't. It's awful. And what's more," he added, ignoring Queen Freda's warning pinch, "what's more, so are you. You haven't changed a bit, Cousin Clive. You're still a great big show-off. I'm tired of all your boasting, and I'm not going to be polite any more, so there!"

Percy and Paula gasped. The Lord Chamberlain dropped his spoon with a clatter. There was a terrible silence. Then:

"You're right," said Cousin Clive, pushing his plate away. "You're absolutely right, old chap. It *is* awful. And I suppose I have been showing off rather. I'm sorry, old chap. I get like that sometimes. It's only because I'm jealous."

"Jealous? You? What of?" asked King Keith, astonished.

"Why, you of course. I mean, there you are with your nice family, all cosy and eating lovely teas in your comfortable palace – and

here I am in this huge place, all on my own
except for lots of bossy servants who never
talk to me. Nobody ever comes to see me,
you know. I don't have many friends. I
suppose it's because I boast so much. I can't
help it. It's a habit I picked up years ago. It
all started with the rattle."

"The rattle?" said everyone wonderingly.

"Yes. Keith was always so clever at making
things," explained Cousin Clive with a sigh.
"Do you remember, Keith? You made your

own rattle. I was terribly impressed. But you wouldn't let me have a go, so I just had to make do with a bought one. And remember the tree house, old chap? I tried to help you build it, but you said I was messing it up and told me to go away. So I ordered a bigger, better one, just to get my own back. Though

I much preferred yours. And you wouldn't
help me make a kite, and I wasn't allowed to
fly yours. . ."

"Is this true, Keith?" asked Queen Freda.
"Wouldn't you share things with Cousin
Clive?"

"Er. . ." said King Keith uncomfortably.
He honestly couldn't remember.

"Shame on you, daddy," said Princess
Paula.

"That's rotten, dad," said Prince Percy.

"I'm surprised at you, Your Majesty," said the Lord Chamberlain.

"Sharing is caring," nodded Doctor Coldfingers wisely. He'd heard that somewhere.

"Anyway, old chap," continued Cousin Clive. "I'm sorry. I'm sorry about boasting, and I'm sorry you've had such a horrible time. If you don't want to be friends with me, I quite understand."

King Keith swallowed hard. Was it true? Had he really refused to share his toys? Was it really the case that Cousin Clive, underneath his swagger, was jealous?

He felt everyone's eyes on him. Cousin Clive seemed to have shrunk, somehow. He was slumped in his seat, poking at his cold cauliflower with a fork, looking rather sad.

"Being humble doesn't suit him, does it?" Princess Paula whispered to Prince Percy.

"I – er – look, I'm sorry too," said King

Keith. "I suppose I was rather a horrid child. And of course I'd like to be friends again."

"Well done, dad," whispered Prince Percy.

"Really?" said Cousin Clive hopefully. "You mean I can come to tea again? You won't mind? You'll put up with my boastful ways?"

"Certainly I will," said King Keith. "If you put up with my stubborn ones. Do you know," he added, "do you know, I rather like the look of this cauliflower. I think I'll try some."

He took a huge spoonful, and popped it in his mouth.

"Mmmmm," said King Keith. "Delicious."

And Cousin Clive beamed. "You really like it?" he said.

"I certainly do," insisted King Keith, and gamely swallowed another mouthful.

And suddenly, everybody was talking. They all agreed that cold cauliflower was one

of the nicest things they had ever tasted. Queen Freda even asked for the recipe. And soon, Cousin Clive was back into his boastful swing again. But that's just the way he was. And nobody minded.

After tea, they all sang songs round the piano, and played charades until they were worn out with laughing. Even the butler joined in. But at last, it was time to go home. Cousin Clive came to the front door, crown askew, and waved as they all got into their shabby old coach.

"You know," said King Keith, when they settled back into the faded cushions. "It was rather nice to see old Clive again. I said I'd pop over tomorrow to show him how to make a crown rack. All right if I bring him back to tea? He's very lonely in that huge palace."

"Of course, dearest," said Queen Freda. "I'll tell Cook to make plenty of red jelly."